soever

LEPRECHAUNS IN DISGUISE

written by
SANDY BARTON

illustrated by
MARK LEISER

Be Brave!
♡ Sandy Barton
2016

To Childhood

THINGS TO DO...

BEFORE YOU READ

Find a comfy place to read, get all snuggly.

Look at the cover. Gather as much information as you can before you start. Get your mind ready for the adventure!

Sometimes it's fun to read with a friend, sometimes it's nice to read alone.

WHILE YOU'RE READING

Make it interesting. Change voices for the different characters. Read parts or the whole thing out loud.

Make a movie in your head as you read. Turn the words into pictures and make them come alive!

Take a few minutes every so often to make predictions. What do you think might happen next?

Remember, predictions are not right or wrong, they just happen or they don't!

WHEN YOU FINISH THE BOOK

Tell a friend or someone in your family about the story - but don't spill the beans, just give them a short summary.

Think about your favorite parts, or your not so favorite parts. What were they and why?

Write a book of your own. Now that's a GREAT adventure!

CONTENTS

LEPRECHAUNS IN DISGUISE

DECISIONS, DECISIONS

Sometimes I try to remember what my life was like before I met Mr. McAllister. And you know what? It's pretty hard to do. If my dog, Sophie, hadn't stuck her nose into Mr. McAllister's home under that huge pine tree, why, none of this would have ever happened! I would have no reason to visit the old woods, I wouldn't have anyone jumping up and down on high branches out of excitement when they see me, I definitely wouldn't have pine cones being dropped on my head from above, and I certainly wouldn't have a magical friendship like I have with my little leprechaun friend!

When I look back at all of our adventures together, I have a tough time deciding which one's my favorite. Was it the discovery? Was it moving all of the leprechauns to the new woods in our van? Was it bringing Mr. McAllister to school for St. Patrick's Day? Was it introducing him to my friend, Miss Gloria, when we had to move away and leave the leprechauns behind? Or was it the frightening rescue in the creek?

There have been so many crazy things that I want to tell you about, and that is why I'm writing another leprechaun book. I want you to have the fun of hearing about my little friends, and I've decided to tell you about one of my all-time favorite adventures with Mr. McAllister... Halloween.

I know, I know — a leprechaun on Halloween seems a little strange, but what hasn't been strange about my friendship with that little man?

Over the past year I have been meeting with lots of kids at schools, and I have asked them which adventure they want to read about next. Their choices were: how Mr. McAllister helped me rescue a baby duckling from the storm sewer, or the time Mr. McAllister went Trick-or-Treating with me. The vote was right smack dab down the middle. Half wanted one, half wanted the other. It looks like I'll have to write two more books!

So, get comfy, and get ready for another leprechaun adventure.

4

HOW MUCH WOOD CAN A SPLUTTER WOMAN CUT?

Shortly after the problem with the kayaks in the creek, life started to calm down. I visited Mr. McAllister every week and we spent lots of lazy summer days talking, building stuff, reading, and chopping wood for winter. I was so happy to be able to help him with that, and the work went much faster with a "big person" around. The whole wood-cutting business was a team effort for sure, and it went something like this:

John, Mr. McAllister's cousin, stood high on the branch of a pine tree. Mr. McAllister and I stood on the ground below waiting for him to cut a limb. John would mumble to himself up there, jumping from branch to branch, and finally find a good one. Then, he would start cutting through the branch with his bow

saw and yell, "Hey old man, move yer ever-lovin' britches out of the way. Here comes a big one!" And, sure enough, a chunk of the branch would come falling down. Now mind you, it wasn't a very big piece. Remember, the leprechaun men are only about ten inches tall, so a piece of firewood that WE think is normal size would smoosh them flat as a pancake! No, the branches that he was cutting were about the size of a hot dog. That's why it was quick work when I helped — I was cutting and splitting that wood like a super-hero. Hmmm, maybe I should call myself Splutter Woman. (It's a mix of splitter and cutter!)

Anyway, we spent a whole day cutting and splitting wood, and we had lots of time to talk when our work was done. John's arms were sore from all of the sawing, so he went home to soak them in a tub of magic ointment made especially for aches and pains. Mr. McAllister and I sat on a log by the pond to watch the dragon flies dive-bomb the bullfrogs. The frogs would give a big "CROAK" and splash into the pond just in time to avoid the dragonflies. I'm not sure if the dragonflies knew that the frogs could eat them for lunch! I think it was a game they must have enjoyed though, because they did it over and over again; what a great place that pond is! It's also the perfect place to just sit and talk, and we did lots of that.

It made me think about when we used to live in the house by the woods, before we moved to the city and had to leave the leprechauns behind. Living in the city makes it a little harder to get together, but he's really not that far away. And I don't mind the trip over because I love talking with Mr. McAllister when it's just the two of us. We can talk about anything at all. Sometimes it's important stuff, sometimes it's not. But talks like that are what help to build a friendship — you learn something new about your friend every time. In fact, that day Mr. McAllister shared something with me that I never knew about him. He seemed almost embarrassed to say it, but he said it anyway. (See... I told you. You can tell a real friend anything!)

"Big One, thank ya for all of the help today. Ya gotta know how grand we think it is that we have all the firewood we need for the winter now. I'll be thankin' ya for the rest of the summer, doncha know. Now we can keep the main fires going all night — every night, and it'll never get too dark. I'm a grown man, yes I am, but there's somethin' I hate to admit. Ya see, I'm, well, I'm uh..." I looked at him and could see his cheeks turning pink, and his eyes were looking down at the ground; he couldn't even look at me, but he continued.

"I'm not a bit proud of it, but... as sure as you're sittin' here, Big One, I'm afraid of the dark, and I always have been. So anything that brings lots of light to the woods is fine with me. I'd be the happiest leprechaun in the world if every one of our houses was lit up with a fire out front, but that wouldn't be safe, now would it?"

I must say, I was surprised to hear that, especially from a man who lives in the woods! If you've ever been in the woods at night you know how dark it can be. I mean DARK. Mr. McAllister said he'd never go out in the woods at night without a whole jar full of fireflies and a pussy willow torch. I tucked that bit of news away in my brain for later. Maybe there was something I could do to help with that problem, and maybe not. I'd have to think about it. All I could think of to say was, "Oh, lots of people are scared of the dark. But don't worry, now you'll have enough wood to keep the fire at the meeting circle burning so you'll feel safe and sound every night." We changed the subject and started cheering for the dragonflies and bullfrogs again.

Before long Miss Gloria came down the pine needle path with a jug of lemonade and some warm chocolate chip cookies — yum! Every time I see her with Mr. McAllister, it makes me so glad that I introduced them to each other. They've been such good friends ever since. So, here she was with her yummy treats, and even she was surprised at how much wood we had stacked that afternoon. Apparently she didn't know the power behind Old Man Britches and Splutter Woman!

SCHOOL DAYS

It wasn't long before the summer days came to an end and the leprechaun kids were getting ready to go back to school. The teachers at the **Day Care Den** were busy getting cribs and cradles ready for the wee ones, and paints and books ready for the older ones. There were lots of new children ready to start school and there was so much to do!

While the teachers were busy inside, the little ones were outside, peeking in the windows to see what was happening in there. Some of the bigger wee ones had figured out how to crawl up onto the mossy roof by going around back and climbing the stairs. From the roof they could peer through the skylights and see right into the Day Care Den — oh what a colorful, exciting place it was!

On the other side of the woods there was much more happening. The cooking school was nearly ready to open its doors, and the gardens around it were bursting with vegetables, herbs and fruit trees. Leprechauns use only the freshest ingredients for their food, and the gardens were much better than any grocery store ever could be.

Not too far from the cooking school was the sewing school. Supplies were coming in daily from all corners of the woods. Baskets of bird feathers hung on the fence, berries waiting to be boiled down for dying cloth filled wooden boxes, and seeds, all sizes and shapes, stuffed bags to overflowing.

Barrels of bunny fur sat ready to be spun into yarn and stuffed into pillows. Bunny fur was everywhere in the woods, and the rabbits were very happy to share whatever extra they had. (There were even boxes around the woods where rabbits could leave fur donations. It was so soft and made the warmest, softest sweaters!)

A little further down the path, the woodworking school was completely ready for students. Boxes of

wooden pegs, tools, and nails were lined up next to the building. Buckets of sticky glue-sap sat ready, and planks of wood were piled high, waiting to be made into something wonderful. There were pieces of pine, lots of pine, oak, birch, walnut, cherry and maple, all with beautiful patterns, lines, rings and swirls.

The teachers, mostly men but some ladies, would show their students how to make spectacular furniture. Many of the cabinets and dressers they made had secret

drawers and hiding places for gold.

The leprechauns had been careful not to cut down too many trees though, and they always planted a new seedling for each tree they took away. It was a good way to keep the woods, woodsy! And besides, they couldn't exactly go to a store to buy wood, now could they?

On the far side of the woods there was, of course, a regular kind of school for leprechaun children; it was where they learned to read, write, do tricky math problems and understand the history of their village. There were very small desks, very small books, very small pencils and very small chairs. In fact everything was very small! And in a week all of the schools would be filled with wee kids fresh from summer vacation.

On the day before school was to start, Mr. McAllister sent Rosie to my house with a message. (As you might remember, Rosie is the beautiful mourning dove who has carried messages between Mr. McAllister and me for years.) She pecked at the window, waited for her treat, and cooed softly as I read the note.

Dear Big One,

Thought you'd be wanting to come for a visit and help us celebrate the first day of school. Not too long ago you talked me into coming with you to your class, doncha know. It's only fair you see what goes on here. There'll be no tricks, and no pine cones dropped on your head. You've got me promise on that. I'll see you at the meeting circle about eight tomorrow morning.

Your friend,

Mr. CW McAllister

I quickly scribbled this note and tied it to Rosie's neck.

Dear Mr. McAllister,

Of course I'll be there! I can't wait to see what the leprechauns' first day of school looks like! See you at eight!

Your friend,

Sandy

Rosie flew off and I ran into the house to make some journals for the kids to use on their first day. This was going to be a fun visit for sure.

PROMISES AND PLEDGES

Early the next morning, I drove over to the woods, stopped in to see Miss Gloria before I went back, and then I followed the path through the trees to the meeting circle. There was a buzz in the air — voices of parents, kids, babies and above them all, I heard Mr. McAllister.

"Ya better be zipping up your lips, we've got a school day to start. And it begins in 3, 2, 1..." Poof! A cloud of gold dust burst out of his hands and before I knew it, the children had tiny bits of gold on their heads, just enough to make them sparkle. They looked at Mr. McAllister and listened very carefully as he spoke.

"Are ya ready?"

"Yes sir"

"Are ya ready?"

"YES SIR!"

"To work hard?"

"YES SIR!"

"To study hard? To say the pledge and the promise?"

"YES SIR!"

"Then repeat after me, me darlins'."

"We promise and pledge..."

"We promise and pledge"

"To be kind to each other..."

"To be kind to each other."

"To listen carefully..."

"To listen carefully"

"And to not play tricks on the teachers..."

"And to not play tricks on the teachers."

"We promise and pledge."

"We promise and pledge."

In an instant they were all singing a school song that sounded like *Twinkle Twinkle Little Star,* but went something like this:

    Summer's over, fall is near,

Honking geese are everywhere.

So it's back to school we'll go,

Learning things we didn't know.

First we'll say our magic words,

Parfney, zoogle, nurpsy, verds.

Parfney, zoogle, nurpsy, verds? I had absolutely no idea what THAT meant, and I had a feeling that I wasn't going to ever know. But it sure sounded funny to me — nurpsy?

Then the coolest thing happened. All of the kids formed a circle around the babies and they held hands. Around and around they went, chanting "Parfney, zoogle, nurpsy, verds. Parfney, zoogle, nurpsy, verds." Faster and faster until in a flash they disappeared. GONE! VANISHED! BYE-BYE!

I stood there with my mouth hanging open trying to figure out what had just happened. Mr. McAllister must have noticed because he came over to me and said,

"Well, Big One, what ya' be thinkin' about that bit

'o magic? Pretty good, doncha think?"

I had to agree that it WAS indeed pretty good.

"W-w-where did they all go?" I asked.

"Oh Big One, do ya have gumballs in your head? What kind of a silly question are ya askin' me now, huh? They went to school, of course. We don't take buses around here."

Wow — that was a first day of school like I've never seen, and I've seen lots of first days, believe me!

IT'S FUN - REALLY IT IS

S ome weeks after school started, I began the gigantic job of getting the garden ready for winter, putting the patio furniture away, and dragging out the Halloween decorations. I LOVE Halloween, so try to imagine all of the stuff I have collected over the years. We have orange lights, white lights, purple lights, drippy candles and creepy lanterns. We have scarecrows on sticks and ghosts that wiggle, witches that glow and cats that hiss. We have pumpkins and straw and scary black spiders. We have spider webs for the bushes and ... well, you get the idea — we have lots of decorations.

We had so much stuff that I decided to take a picture of it to show Mr. McAllister. I knew he'd think it was pretty crazy, and I was quite sure he had never celebrated Halloween. (But then I thought what an adorable

Halloween parade that would be... all of those wee folks dressed up in costumes!) When I finished decorating, I took a few pictures and drove over to show my little friend how the house looked.

It was a beautiful fall afternoon in the woods, the kind that makes you want to be outside all day. The smell of wood fires swirled around my nose; I kept breathing in that delicious aroma. The late afternoon sunlight was painting golden lines between the trees as if lasers were slicing through the air. And the maples and oaks had already begun to lay their blanket of leaves on top of a bed of pine needles. Such a quiet, musty, magical place it was. No wonder the leprechauns loved it so much.

"Mr. McAllister! Mr. McAllister! Are you back here? I have something to show you."

Silence. Plop, plop — down came the pine cones on my head, just as I expected, but for some reason I'm always surprised. Sticky pinecones, hanging from my hair — ahhh, such a lovely way to be greeted.

"I was hopin' you'd be comin' by today. A beauty of a day it is, doncha think, Big One?"

"Oh, it's beautiful alright. That's why I came over. I've been working on our Halloween decorations all day and I just had to show you a few pictures." We sat on the tree stumps at the meeting circle while Mr. McAllister examined the pictures.

As he looked at them, his face got very serious and he began to rub his beard.

"Ya say that you've put all of this outside?"

"Yep."

"Are these spider webs on the bushes?"

"Yep."

"Why?"

"To look scary!"

"Who are you trying to scare, Big One?"

"The kids."

"Why?"

"Because that's what you do on Halloween night ... scare people."

"Why?"

"Um, well, 'cause, it's fun!"

"OH, IT'S FUN TO SCARE LITTLE KIDS? WHAT KIND OF A MEAN WOMAN ARE YA, BIG ONE?"

"I'm not mean, that's just what happens on Halloween. It's a spooky, fun night and everyone expects to get a little scared. Hey, YOU like to play silly tricks on people, so it's not that much different."

"I may like to play tricks, but not scary tricks... and NEVER in the dark! I'd be scarin' meself if I tried that!"

Oh, there it was again — that new bit of information I had tucked away in my brain. Mr. McAllister was afraid of the dark. He'd never understand how much fun

Halloween can be if he's terrified of the dark.

"Mr. McAllister, do you like candy?"

"By golly, now I'm sure you have gumballs in your head, Big One. What a silly question. No, I don't like candy. I LOVE candy!"

"Well do you like to pretend?"

"Pretend what?"

"Pretend to be animals or people or things?"

"Oh Big One, I do think you've been working too hard. Ya askin' me if I like to pretend to be 'things'? Are ya getting a little kooky?" He looked at me as if I were from another planet. Then he took my hand in his. "Big One, are ya feelin' ok? What exactly are ya talking about?"

Explaining Halloween to a leprechaun is a difficult thing. You dress up in costumes that might be "things" — like a bottle of catsup or a TV (silly). Or you use fake make-up and turn yourself into something gross that would scare the pants off of you on any other day of the year (this makes no sense). You beg for candy from people you don't know (not good manners). You eat WAY too much junk food in one night (not good for your belly). You stay up way past your bedtime (not good for your teachers the next day). You have so much sugar in your body that you are bouncing off the walls when you finally get home (definitely not good for your teeth, your parents or your teachers).

Yes, trying to convince Mr. McAllister that all of those things were actually what made Halloween fun, was harder than I thought, but he seemed fascinated. The only thing he really didn't like was the part about all of this taking place in the dark. That freaked him out more than a little bit.

"Big One, doncha think Halloween would be more fun during the day. You could see where yer walking, and it wouldn't be so blasted scary."

"No, no no. That would never work. It has to be dark; it's just better that way, trust me."

"Well you can be sure that you'll never catch me runnin' around in the dark, beggin' for me life to get candy from a whole neighborhood of big people, who are just waitin' to scare the britches off of me! No, you'll be waitin' for pigs to fly before ya see me doin' that, me friend."

And that's when it hit me – I just HAD to take Mr. McAllister Trick-or-Treating with me. How funny would that be?

ROLLERCOASTERS
AND REASONS WHY

It was three weeks before Halloween and I finally got up the courage to ask Mr. McAllister to come with me Trick-or-Treating. I knew he would love it if he gave it a try, but I wasn't so sure I could talk him into it. I also knew that it wasn't so much about dressing up, eating candy and getting scared; it was more about the dark. You know how it feels to be afraid of something; it doesn't matter how many people tell you it's not scary, it's scary to you, and that's all you need to know. But sometimes, if you're very brave, you agree to try something if you have someone to do it with you.

That's how it was when my best friend talked me into going on the biggest rollercoaster at Crystal Beach. If you rode the Comet, you were brave. You were a big

31

kid. You proved that you could do anything... well, almost! I remember climbing into the front car, yes the front car, ready to do it. My hands were all sweaty, my heart was beating so fast, and I was terrified. The guy buckled us in, pulled down the bar that kept us from flying across the sky, and laughed as he said, "Ok girls, enjoy the ride." The way he said it made me want to get out right then and there, but my friend grabbed my wrist and said, "Sandy, this is gonna be the coolest thing ever."

As the coaster crawled up the first hill, slowly, very slowly, I could hear every click from the chain below that was pulling us up. UGH! I couldn't even breathe. We finally made it to the top and it just stopped and teetered long enough for me to think that this was a horrible idea. My eyes had been squeezed shut for the whole slow climb up, and while we teetered (it seemed like hours, but it was really only a few seconds) I opened my eyes. Yikes! I could see the lake below, and all of the people watching us, looking like tiny ants. Before I knew it -ahhhhhhhhhhhhhhhhhhhhhhhhhhhhhhhh we were diving down that hill faster than the speed of light, racing so fast, and I was holding my breath the whole way. My scream got stuck in my throat, so all I could do was grit my teeth and hold on for dear life. Then we were up again, then down, then around curves and under tunnels.

My stomach flipped, then flopped, then flipped again. I might have even caught a bug between my front teeth, I can't remember. We finally came to a screeching stop a few minutes later and it was over. Just like that. It was the most fun thing I had ever done. Yep. Something that I was so afraid to do five minutes before, turned out to be AWESOME! So awesome, that we went on the Comet four more times that day. A best friend makes some of the scariest times ok just by being there with you. That's what I thought about as I considered spending Halloween with Mr. McAllister. I would try to convince him that it would be ok, and maybe even AWESOME! So off I went on another leprechaun mission.

My little friend was making new torches when I found

him in the woods. He was whistling and doing a jig, so I knew he was in a good mood.

"Well if it isn't Mean Woman Big One — She who scares kids and decorates with creepy stuff." He chuckled when he said it, so I knew he was only teasing me.

"You'd better beware of my pet spider! And oh, my pumpkin's got fangs, so you'd better watch out for him, too."

"Aw don't be tryin' to scare me, Big One. I got me own tricks I can play on you if you don't watch out!"

"I know all about your tricks. Hey, aren't you just a little bit curious about Halloween?"

"Curious, yes. Do I want to do it, NO!"

"Oh, but wouldn't it be fun to dress up and collect more candy than you could eat in a year?"

"To be sure. Fun, delicious and doncha know, a dream come true. But do I have to be repeating myself again? It's not something I'd be lovin' to do in the dark. Now, come help me deliver these torches to Patrick, John and Alanah. They used their last ones over the weekend."

As we walked I had a chance to talk Mr. McAllister into at least thinking about it. I told him I'd be with him the whole time, we'd have a flashlight, and we'd only go on streets with streetlights. That made him feel a tiny bit better. By the time we finished delivering the torches, it was dinner time and I had to get home. My brave little friend made a pinky promise that he'd think about Halloween and let me know in the morning. I had a good feeling about this, and with any luck I'd have a buddy to go Trick-or-Treating with on October 31st!

ROSIE'S REPORT

I was finishing my breakfast when I heard Rosie's coos at the window; she was there to bring Mr. McAllister's decision. Her tan and gray feathers were so beautiful against the sky, and I couldn't help but think how lucky we were to have such a kind mourning dove who would fly back and forth between our homes to deliver important messages. It was a cloudy day and a little chill was in the air, so I put my slippers on and a snuggly hoodie and went out to see her. Of course I brought her a handful of her favorite seeds and carefully untied the message while she pecked at the morning treat.

Dear Big One,

It's against everything I know to be sensible, and a

very big chance to be takin' even with me best friend.

I've spent the night tossin' and turnin' about this Halloween idea. I know ya wouldn't want me to do something dangerous, and ya wouldn't do anything to make fun of me, but I have to say that I'm not excited about the plan. I hope you understand why I don't want to be out in the dark gettin' scared out of my britches. No, I don't want to go out on Halloween... but I will because you are my best friend and you will make sure it's ok, won't you, Big One? Since I have never done this kind of craziness before, you'll have to choose a good costume for me. And don't be thinkin' of dressin' me up as a lady leprechaun. And no blood! And no fangs! Please come for a visit so we can figure this Halloween thing out. I'm trustin' you Big One, I'm trustin' you a lot, doncha know. Boo! Ha! Did I scare ya?

Your friend,

Mr. McAllister

Oh my goodness! He was going to do it! I was jumping all over the yard, looking a little silly, but who cares? I was so happy. I wrote a quick note telling him that I was happy he was going to give it a try, and yes, he would have a super fun time. And yes, he could trust me. Then I rolled up the message and tied it to Rosie. Off she went over the trees and back to the woods. Now it was my job to make Mr. McAllister calm and maybe even a little excited about Halloween. I had an idea, so off to the market I went.

Flowers and pumpkins, corn stalks and vegetables, and lots of people were at the market. I went to my favorite farm stand and found just what I was looking for — little orange gourds. You've probably seen them before. They look like tiny pumpkins except they're a little smaller than a baseball. I thought they'd be the perfect size for leprechaun Jack-o-lanterns and just the thing to get Mr. McAllister pumped up about Halloween. If I went over and showed him how to carve one, he could help the others, and before long the whole woods would be decorated with leprechaun-sized pumpkins! Of course the farmer asked me how many gourds I wanted, and when I said 100 he almost fell over.

"One hundred? One hundred gourds?"

"Yes, sir, one hundred."

"Do you want a box or are you going to stuff them into your pockets?"

"How many pockets do you think I have?" I asked. He laughed and we both started filling the box. "2,4,6,8,10... 42, 44, 46... 96, 98, 100!"

"So, if you don't mind me asking, what are you going to do with all of these?"

"Oh, I'm going to give them to my leprechaun friends." I knew he wouldn't believe me, so it was a safe thing to say.

"Ha! That's a good one. Your leprechaun friends, huh? Maybe they can fill them with gold. Leprechaun friends. Lady, you're funny!"

I paid him and walked to my car — very slowly. That box was sure heavy! It felt like there was a load of bricks in there, but I made it, put them in the trunk and drove home.

That night I went to see Mr. McAllister and I took with

me a box of 100 gourds, a little knife, and a few good
ideas for his costume. This was going to be interesting.

ITTY-BITTY
JACK-O-LANTERNS

I managed to get to the woods a few hours before it got dark so we would have plenty of time to work. That box was so heavy though, I had to bring a wagon with me. Miss Gloria saw me coming and came out to see what in the world I was up to now. When I told her about the gourds, she jumped at the chance to join us.

"Oh I'd love to help with the carving, do you think they would mind if I came back, too? Let me run in and get a knife and some cookies and then we can go. Don't move a muscle, I'll be right back." In a jiffy she returned with an apron on, a bowl filled with chocolate chip cookies, a knife and a marker. "They'll want to draw their faces on before they carve, especially if they never did this before!"

Leave it to Miss Gloria to think of everything.

We were greeted by several dropping pine cones and, "Hello lovely lassies. What have ya got draggin' in the wagon?" Before we could answer, he spotted the cookies. "Well, if it isn't the pot o'gold of cookies! Mind if I have one?"

"That's why I brought them! Help yourself!" Miss Gloria handed over the bowl and Mr. McAllister took one cookie in each hand.

"I'll be tellin' ya a secret, but ya best not be tellin' anybody I said so. Miss Gloria, your cookies are delicious. Better than my Mrs. can make. But shhhh. Don't ya dare tell her. I'd hate to hurt her feelings. If she heard me say that, she'd dump a bucket of water on me head, sure as I'm talkin. Thank you for the treat. So, Big One, what's in the wagon?"

"These are gourds and they are going to be your Halloween decorations back here in the woods. We're going to..."

"Decorations? In these woods? Why do I want a

bunch of orange things back here?"

"Oh, wait till you see what we are going to do with them. You'll love it because they'll light up the woods!" When he heard that, Mr. McAllister nearly lit up himself. I had a feeling he'd like the idea of making the woods not quite so dark. So we went to work unloading all of the gourds and were finally ready to draw faces.

"So, tell me again what you're wantin' me to do?"

"Well, you draw a face on the side of this gourd. You can make it scary or funny, or whatever you want. Then you cut around the stem and take off the top — kind of like a hat."

"But isn't it a bunch of mushy glop inside? That's where the seeds would be, Big One."

"Oh, I know. That's the best part. The gooey, gloppy seeds! And I'll need your help with that part."

"That's fine. I like to help."

Little did he know that he'd have to stick his hand into the guts to clean out the seeds. His hand was small enough to do that.

So Mr. McAllister drew a face on his gourd. He decided on triangle eyes, a round nose and a wide smile with only three teeth — one on top, two on the bottom. He thought it was the funniest thing he had ever seen. That gave me hope that he was really, really going to like Halloween! I cut the top and slowly pulled it off. The slimy strings of goop and seeds laid on the ground while I looked at Mr. McAllister.

"Ok, go ahead."

"Go ahead what?"

"Go ahead and stick your hand in there to clean it out."

"Me? Stick my hand in there? Are ya out of your ever lovin' mind? You DO have   gumballs in yer head, Big One. That's slimy, doncha know!"

"You said you wanted to help, so it's time to help." He looked at me with a really funny face and slowly pushed his shirt sleeve up past his elbow. Then he began to put his hand in, but pulled it out before it ever got near the slime. "You'd be kiddin' me about this, right?"

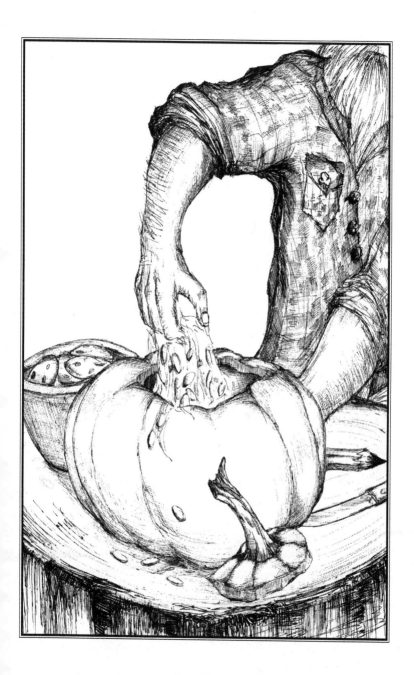

47

"Nope. Not kidding. Go ahead." He held his breath as if he were going under water or something, (or as if he were going down the big hill on a rollercoaster) and he did it. Stuck his hand in clear up to his elbow. His face changed from funny to scared and then to grossed out. I couldn't help but laugh. Then Miss Gloria started laughing. And before long, even Mr. McAllister was laughing so hard he had tears coming down his cheeks.

"This is disgusting. This is slimy. This is the most fun I've had in a week!"

It wasn't long before the inside was cleaned out and he was ready to carve. After a few instructions, he had the hang of it and he carved a perfect little Jack-o-lantern. He named it Fred. Fred O'Malley. And Fred had a place of honor next to the McAllisters' front door. "He's a handsome lad, he is. Couldn't be better. Nice to meet ya, Fred."

"Oh yes he could be even nicer," I said. "Run in and get a torch please. You'll see what I mean." I broke off the end of the torch, stuck it inside the pumpkin and lit it. I wish you could have seen Mr. McAllister's face when he saw Fred glowing! His eyes got big and he started to laugh and dance and clap his hands. He made such a commotion that his family and friends came out of their homes to see what was happening.

At first they were scared, but Mr. McAllister yelled, "Come closer! Meet me new friend, Fred O'Malley. He's gonna light up the woods, doncha know! You can all have a Fred 'cause Sandy brought 100 of them just for us! Here, follow me and you can be choosin' your own. I'll show ya how to carve them and Miss Gloria will help. Happy Halloween!"

He danced down the path to the pile of 99 gourds. We could hear him singing all the way. Here was my wee friend who was afraid of Halloween and then found something about it he loved. I felt that we had won a little victory with Fred. Now to plan a costume for a leprechaun who's ten inches tall.

UNLEASH THE MAGIC

It was kind of tough trying to pull the new fan of Halloween from the carving party. Mr. McAllister was having a ball going from table to table checking out the faces, and talking his friends into not being afraid of the slimy guts. Now he was Mr. Brave! It was funny to hear him.

"Oh don't ya be a little cry baby about gettin' your hands a wee bit slimy. It's only seeds, doncha know. They won't bite ya. I did it meself and I didn't put up a fuss!" Hmmm, that wasn't exactly true, but I didn't want to embarrass him and tell them what really happened! So Miss Gloria and I did what we could to help and were happy to see everyone getting excited about Halloween. After all, that's what we hoped would happen. Finally I pulled Mr. McAllister aside and asked if we could talk about his costume before I had to leave. I could tell he would have rather kept carving and chatting with the others, but we sat out in front of his house for a while and got it settled.

"Now Big One, I don't understand why we can't be happy about the Jack-o-lanterns and leave it at that. Why do you think I have to go Trick-or-Treating, too?"

"Well, there are lots of reasons. You'll love getting all of that candy. You'll love seeing all of the costumes. And it will feel good to do something you might be a little afraid to do... walk around the neighborhood in the dark. Just think, it will be the first time in your life that you can be in the middle of hundreds of big people and they won't even know you're a leprechaun! How cool is that?"

"I said I would go, and I will be keepin' my word, but what is your idea for my costume? I must say, you've got me wonderin' that!"

"Well, I think I've got the perfect plan. What if you're a cowboy?"

"A cowboy, ya say? And how do you suggest I do that?"

"Well, do you have boots?"

"I do."

"Do you have long pants?"

"I do"

"A vest?"

"I have lots of vests."

"How about a plaid shirt with a bandana for around your neck?"

"Let me see. If it's a plaid shirt ya need, yes. But why would I be wearing a banana around my neck?"

"Not a banana, a bandana. It's a handkerchief that cowboys sometimes wear around their necks, but I'm not sure why. They just do. Besides, I have one you can borrow."

"And that's all I'll be needin?"

"Um no. You'll need a cowboy hat, spurs for your boots, and a pretend gun."

"I'll be using NO gun. No gun, do ya hear me? And

spurs, what are they?"

"I said a pretend gun — a water gun will work if we can find a super small one. And spurs are pointy things that go on the back of your boots. Cowboys use them to make their horses go faster. OH MY GOODNESS— YOU NEED A HORSE!"

"Have ya lost your mind, Big One? I am not getting a horse! Besides, where would I get a horse, anyway?"

"If I'm not mistaken, you chased a 'Big Red Horse' out of your house with a broom the first day I met you. Remember?"

"Remember? As sure as I'm sittin' here, I remember! But ya don't mean. Nah. You can't be serious. Not Sophie?"

"Sophie."

"But she's no horse, she's a dog!"

"I know, but she'd make a great horse for you to ride, and everyone would think you were part of Sophie's costume. I could make some reins and a saddle and I could lead her around just like she's my little pony!"

"A little pony with a little cowboy ridin' on her back? Ha! Well if that doesn't put the sparkle in the gold. You're a smart one, you are. Ok, you've got yourself a deal. An Irish cowboy I'll be, with a banana around my neck."

"A bandana. Not a banana," I laughed, but it was no use. He was already on his way back to join the others, and I heard him mumbling about horses and bananas. Silly little leprechaun.

The sky was growing dark and soon I'd be leaving, but before I did, I was hoping to see all of the Jack-o-lanterns lit up. Just as I turned to ask Mr. McAllister if they were going to light them, he disappeared — then reappeared on a high branch, and made the announcement.

"I can't believe me eyes. It's a sea of orange in our woods. A good job you've done with this Halloween decorating, but the real test will be when we light them up! Take them back to your homes and wait for my signal. Then make some magic happen!" They all cheered and hurried away with their "Freds". I looked around as the woods suddenly became speckled with orange, as if polk-a-dots had invaded.

"Psssssst... Mr. McAllister."

"What is it Big One?"

"You forgot to tell them to put a torch inside."

"Doncha be worrying about that. We're leprechauns, have ya forgotten?"

"But..."

"Unleash the magic!" With that the woods were glowing with 100 tiny Jack-o-lanterns, each one with a different face. There were grins and frowns, eyes and noses of every shape and size, and no torches inside. Leprechaun magic somehow made them light up and glow as if they were filled with gold. What a sight it was. Halloween had come to life in the woods.

SPECTACULAR SPURS

It seemed to me that Miss Gloria could do anything. She could sew, she could cook, she could garden and she made the most beautiful Christmas stockings I ever did see. Each year before Christmas she would make her grandchildren new stockings to hang for Santa to fill. She lovingly sewed the edges. She carefully sewed their names. But it was the way she made them sparkle that was so amazing. Miss Gloria glued and sewed hundreds of beads and sequins on each one, and oh how they came to life!

Thinking about those stockings made me think of shiny silver spurs for cowboy McAllister. I wondered if Miss Gloria could make spurs for the costume... not just any spurs, but the most sparkly, glittery spurs ever made! After all, it wasn't every day that a leprechaun went Trick-

or-Treating. This called for the best of everything, so I stopped at Miss Gloria's house on my way home.

"Spurs? What in the world do you need spurs for dear? Are you taking a trip out west?"

"No, nothing like that," I said. "I need them for Mr. McAllister. He's going to be a cowboy for Halloween."

"A cowboy? A cowboy? He's going out Trick-or-Treating? Where? How?"

"Yep, a cowboy. He's going to use Sophie for a horse. I'm going to take him to my house and he can go around our neighborhood. Can you just imagine how funny that will be?"

"Funny? It will be hysterical!"

"So, do you think you can make spurs, Miss Gloria? And make them sparkle like the Christmas stockings?"

"Of course I can! Oh this will be fun, my dear. I'll get started on them in the morning. Spurs! I'm making a leprechaun a pair of spurs. My life went from boring to crazy just like that!" She snapped her fingers to show me how fast things changed. She was right. Life is far from boring when you know leprechauns.

RIDE 'EM COWBOY

"What time can we leave?"

"As soon as you're dressed, cowboy."

"And we're going to Trick-or-Treat on your street?"

"Sure 'nuf, partner."

"What in blazes does that mean?"

"Oh, that's cowboy talk. Are you almost ready?"

"Hold your horses, Big One."

He was laughing so hard at his own joke that I actually heard him snort! Miss Gloria and I had been standing outside his door for about fifteen minutes while he finished getting his costume on. The plan was for me to drive him to our house, get Sophie ready, then head on out to Trick-or-Treat. I couldn't wait much longer to see him. He was going to look so good as a wee cowboy. The door creaked open and out he stepped.

"How do I look?"

I wasn't ready for what I saw. There in front of me was Mr. McAllister, the perfect cowboy, only ten inches tall. I didn't know whether to laugh or cry or hug him or jump for joy, so I did it all. I swept him up and gave him a big hug, danced with him for a minute, then put him down while I took another look.

His boots were a shiny brown. The jeans were just the right amount of worn-out, and the chaps he wore over the jeans were brown leather with fringe down the side. (Luckily I found a store that sold doll clothing, and one of their bigger dolls was almost the exact same size and shape as Mr. McAllister. I had to do a little adjusting with my sewing machine, but not much.) He had chosen his blue plaid shirt and for once he tucked it in. That allowed his belt with the HUGE rodeo belt buckle to stand out on his chubby belly.

I had found a very small silver squirt gun that fit nicely into the holster — he was quite thrilled with that! The bandana, well, he put over his mouth and looked like he was planning to rob a bank. As he explained it to me, it would hide his beard and he wouldn't look so much like a leprechaun.

But it was the cowboy hat that made me almost fall on the ground laughing. It was a tall one, high on his head, but his head was so small that it came down to his eyebrows.

"Howdy ma'am. Right nice to meet you," he said tipping his hat and bowing his head a bit.

"I curtsied and said, "Howdy, cowboy. Right nice to meet you, too."

"Ma'am," he said as he leaned over to look at Miss Gloria. "Whacha got in the bag? More cookies? I reckon I could eat one or two before I leave."

"No. These, sir, are your spurs," she said and held the bag out in front of her. I could tell by her smile that she was very excited for Mr. McAllister to see them.

He took the bag and carefully unfolded the top. He peeked inside — his eyes lit up like the Fourth of July! "Oh my good gracious have ya ever seen anything the likes of these? He pulled the spurs out of the bag and held them up. They're brighter than me very own gold, they are!" Every inch of the metal spurs was covered with something that sparkled. In fact, they were so sparkly that the three of us had to squint our eyes — why it was almost like looking at the sky on a very sunny day! Miss Gloria is a genius.

Mr. McAllister sat on the ground and we joined him. He stuck his left foot up in the air as Miss Gloria attached the spurs to his boot, then the right foot. His costume was complete; he was officially a cowboy. There was only one thing left to do. Mr. McAllister hugged Miss Gloria's ankles, said thank you a bazillion times, and we were off.

We waved good-bye to the others as they eagerly stood on branches to get a good view of their fearless leader, leaving for a night of Halloween fun. The pumpkins were glowing, the owls were hooting, darkness was falling like a curtain, and the moon was already casting shadows in the woods. I have to admit it was a little spooky. I reminded him it would be ok, and he reminded me that he had a squirt gun and would protect me. I'm thinking he was feeling a wee bit braver than normal. Maybe it was his costume, maybe it was because we were together, but as we climbed into the car and headed for my house, I knew one thing for sure — it was going to be a memorable night!

CANDY, CANDY AND MORE CANDY

Driving across town with Mr. McAllister strapped in and dressed as a cowboy was pretty funny. He changed the radio stations a million times in the twenty minutes it took to get to my house, and decided he liked the country station the best. It did go with his costume, and I caught him bouncing around in his seat more than once. What a character he is!

My family was anxiously waiting for us to get there and they came running when we pulled in the driveway. They hadn't seen Mr. McAllister in a while and were quite surprised when a cowboy jumped out of the car. There was lots of hugging and chattering as we walked up to the front door, and then came the terrifying scream.

"Get me out of here! Run for your lives — there's a

gigantic orange monster at your door. Quick get back in the car before it eats us alive! Run!!!!!!"

I caught him, got on my knees and looked him in the eyes.

"Mr. CW McAllister. It's ok! Calm down. Take a good look at what you're running away from. It's another Fred, just bigger. That's our pumpkin with a scary, mean face. Turn around and take a look. Really. It's ok." Slowly he turned around and saw that the gigantic orange monster was just another Fred.

"Oh, Big One, me heart is racing like a train. That thing almost scared the britches off of me, doncha know. Is the whole night gonna be this scary?"

"Well, you'll probably see things that are creepy, but try to remember it's all pretend. Everybody has costumes, and everybody will be bigger than you, so you do have to be prepared for that. If you know what to expect, maybe it won't be so scary for you. Are you ok now?"

"I am. I just wasn't expectin' to meet such a big Fred, is all. I am ok. I am ok."

Sophie was in the living room wagging her tail and gave Mr. McAllister a big sloppy kiss. She was happy to see he was carrying a squirt gun and not a pine needle broom!

"Ok gang, this is it. Time to saddle up our pony and go out Trick-or-Treating."

The kids were already in their costumes and were going to go out with their friends. My husband was going to stay home and pass out candy, and I was dressed as a cowgirl. We were almost ready. The leather saddle that I made fit comfortably on Sophie's back and she stood still while I tied it around her belly. The saddle bags hung down from it and would be great for holding the candy. Then I attached the reins and gave Mr. McAllister a boost into the saddle. It was a sight I will never, ever forget. He looked fabulous.

"Hold on tight, partner. Ride 'em cowboy!" In a flash I led my horse and rider out the door and into the night, the dark night. And guess who didn't even notice that it was dark out? Yep, Mr. McAllister. He was so busy looking at everybody's costumes and decorations that he wasn't scared even one little bit.

The first house we went to had a front lawn loaded with ghosts and goblins, graveyards and spooky music. They even had smoke coming from their bushes! I whispered to Mr. McAllister that it was all pretend and he whispered back that he was ok. I was so proud of how brave he was being.

"Trick-or-Treat!" I yelled and rang the bell.

"Well what do we have here?" the lady asked as she opened the door with her huge bowl of candy.

"Oh, hi!" I answered. I'm a cowgirl and this is my horse."

"And I like that handsome cowboy doll that's riding your horse. Where did you ever find such a thing?"

"Oh, he's a friend, not a doll. A little friend."

"Ha! A friend. Sure he is." The lady looked at the cowboy on Sophie's back and kept looking, trying to figure out what kind of a friend he might be. Mr. McAllister tipped his hat at her and said, "Howdy ma'am.

Right nice to meet ya."

The lady almost fainted. She thought he was fake. "Here. Take all the candy you want." She never took her eyes off him. She look terrified!

Mr. McAllister tipped his hat again and said, "Thank you kindly, ma'am."

I took the reins, led Sophie down the driveway and walked away. I heard a giggle, then a laugh, then the biggest laugh that ever came from a ten inch man. I looked at him and I started laughing, too.

"Oh, Big One, that lady was more scared of me than I ever was of anything in my life. Did ya see her face when I tipped my hat? It was a good one, doncha think?"

"Yep. You scared her all right! That was so funny! And that was just our first house!"

"Well what are ya waitin' for, Big One. Let's go to another."

We went to every house on the block, and at each one of them, the people were completely confused about the little cowboy. He sat still as a statue until they held out the bowl of candy. Then he'd reach over, take some, put it in the saddlebag, tip his hat and say a little something. That's when they'd stare, get all nervous, and make faces that let us know we had done a good job of scaring them.

I'd say the best scaring we did was when two boys came running past us on the sidewalk and then stopped dead in their tracks. They looked back at Sophie, then at Mr. McAllister. Slowly they started coming towards us with big smiles on their faces. Not friendly smiles... mean ones.

"What's that supposed to be?" they asked pointing at Sophie.

"A horse," I said.

"Looks like a dog to me," said the one kid. I had a feeling this was not going to end well.

"Yea, and what's that supposed to be on its back?" asked the other kid.

"A cowboy." They burst out laughing. I could see Mr. McAllister was not pleased.

"What are ya thinkin' is so blasted funny, lads?" he

yelled. The boys stopped laughing when they heard the cowboy talk. I didn't know what would happen next, but when I saw what they did, I almost screamed.

"What, does it have batteries or something?" the biggest kid laughed and grabbed Mr. McAllister by the holster and held him up in the air. Those little cowboy boots were moving so fast they were just a brown blur, but the spurs- oh how they sparkled and flashed in the moonlight!

"Put me down you overgrown piece of cabbage! Put me down, I tell ya!"

"Come on — how does this thing work?" the kid screamed, lifting the back of Mr. McAllister's vest to look for batteries.

"Looking for this?" Mr. McAllister screamed, and in a flash he opened his hands right in front of the boy's face and POOF! Mr. McAllister disappeared and left the boy standing there holding a HUGE hairy spider.

"Ahhhhhhhh. Get it off me! Help! I hate spiders!" He dropped it to the ground and the two boys ran away screaming.

I couldn't believe what I had just seen. All I could do was watch the boys running and screaming all through the neighborhood, and then look down at the spider. But it wasn't a spider for long. Before I knew it, BAM! A flash of light, and there was the cowboy back on his horse, ready to go to the next house.

"How did you... what just... yikes!"

"Have ya forgotten, Big One, I've got a wee bit of magic of me own to use! That was what ya call leprechaun Trick-Without-a-Treat, doncha know. Ha! I'm lovin' this Halloween, I am!"

Mr. McAllister was having such a good time he didn't want to stop. He played a few more tricks on people, nothing bad, but tricky enough to make Halloween interesting for the people passing out candy.

At one house Mr. McAllister made a scarecrow dance on the front lawn. The man inside yelled to his wife, "Doris, quick, you gotta see this!" When Doris came to the door, the scarecrow ran up to her and hugged her.

Well, that lady screamed and slammed the door so fast, the whole house shook. And I laughed so hard I fell on the ground. I could hardly breathe.

Another time we were just leaving a house and a little girl dressed as a bumble bee was coming up the driveway. She stumbled, fell down and dropped all of her candy in the mud. Mr. McAllister looked at me as if to say, "Should I?" and I nodded. Sure, why not.

With a wave of his hand an enormous stream of candy started falling from the tree and piled up in her bag until it overflowed. The little girl's eyes stared at the bag in disbelief. Her mom stared at the bag in disbelief. As for us? We just walked past her and said, "Happy Halloween Little Bumble Bee!"

Mr. McAllister was having such fun and it made me so happy. But it was getting late and the saddlebags were getting full, so we decided to head for home. That's when disaster struck.

OFF TO THE RACES

We had visited 46 houses and were turning the corner to go home when something jumped out of the bushes right in front of us. It was a cat, a big, black cat. It hissed, arched its back and then swiped at Sophie's face. Luckily it missed her, but it really made her mad. The cat took off running and Sophie took off after the cat. The reins were torn from my hands. I barely had enough time to scream, "Sophie stop. Sophie!!!! Hold on for your life Mr. McAllister! Don't let go!"

I started chasing after the dog who was chasing after the cat, trying with all my might to catch them. In all of the excitement, Mr. McAllister kicked his boots and the spurs went against Sophie's sides, which made her run even faster. What a disaster.

Little kids were screaming as parents pulled them out of the way of the racing dog with the wee cowboy hanging on for dear life. I was running past shocked families screaming, "I'm so sorry. I'm so sorry. Sorry about that. I'm trying to catch them. Oops, sorry."

I was nearly close enough to grab the reins when I heard a voice with an Irish accent yelling, "Giddy-up! Faster, Sophie, let's get it." Well, the chase went on for an entire block and a half before I finally caught them. I was out of breath, my legs were all wobbly, and I couldn't believe my eyes. They had cornered the cat. Mr. McAllister was standing next to Sophie, squirt gun out, and he gave the cat one long soaking. Cats don't like water much, and that big black cat disappeared into the night.

"Well, Big One, that was quite a ride doncha know. This big red horse can really run. And bless my lucky stars, I see what you mean about the spurs; I remembered what ya said about them. I kicked them into Sophie's sides and she took off faster than a leprechaun on a gold hunt! I'd be thinkin' that she's the fastest animal alive, I would!"

I was still trying to catch my breath; I was exhausted. "What do you say we go home. It's been quite a night."

"Aww, go home so soon? I'm thinkin' the fun is just beginning."

"No, that's enough fun for one night. Time to get you home, partner."

He hugged my ankles, I patted him on the ten gallon hat, and we both had a good laugh. Sophie was taking a rest on the ground eating a candy bar, and my brave little cowboy put his squirt gun back into the holster and climbed back in the saddle. He could get on himself when Sophie was lying down on the ground. I led them back down the street; by now most of the kids were tired and were heading home too.

Back at the house my kids showed Mr. McAllister how they counted and sorted their candy. Our two saddlebags held 113 pieces of candy, and Mr. McAllister proudly announced he was going to eat all of it himself. After considering the size of the bellyache I told him he'd have, he decided against that and said he'd share it with the clan.

Hearing him tell my family about his wild ride was almost as funny as seeing it happen in person. And you know what? Not once did he mention the dark, or being afraid – not once. He may be little, but he is very big on bravery! We both agreed it was the best Halloween ever. Well, it was his first Halloween, so it had to be the best, but it was my best Halloween for sure. I loved seeing my friend do something he was afraid to try, and show lots of courage besides. Best of all, he had fun doing it. I couldn't help but think that Halloween with a leprechaun might be even more fun than St. Patrick's Day. But don't ever tell a leprechaun that!

STORIES AROUND
THE CAMPFIRE

The cowboy fell asleep in the car on the way home. There was no changing radio stations, there was no playing with the windows, and there was no bouncing to the music ... only snoring. **VERY LOUD SNORING.** And I do think there was a bit of dreaming mixed in. He was moving his hands and feet and saying things like "Faster... good gumballs... hey... take that... water..."

"Wake up, we're home. Mr. McAllister, wake up." I had to shake him a few times before his eyes opened, just below the brim of his hat.

"Huh? What? Where?"

"We're home, wake up sleepy head."

"Doncha know I wasn't sleeping. I was just resting me eyes."

"Oh, ok. Resting your eyes? Do you snore when you rest your eyes?"

"Don't be saying' that I was snoring'. I don't snore. Never have. Never will."

"If you say so."

Our walk into the woods was very, very dark. The moon was hidden by the clouds that covered the sky. But as soon as we got near to the village, the beautiful orange glow of the Jack-o-lanterns lit up the paths and reminded us how good it feels to go somewhere new, and how wonderful it feels to come back home again.

A fire was burning at the meeting circle and everyone was waiting to hear all about Mr. McAllister's first Halloween. Miss Gloria was there too, knowing that her new little friend must have a big story to tell. And did he ever!

We all listened as he stood on a tree stump and told the tales. The warm light of the fire made his eyes dance as he described the ride across town, the huge orange monster that almost scared the britches off of him, the lady who thought he was fake, the ghosts and witches, the monsters and princesses. Of course he had to tell about his brief time as a big hairy spider, the candy that rained from the tree, the sneaky black cat that jumped from the bushes, the big red horse that ran faster than lightning, the magic spurs, and the brave cowboy who saved the day with his squirt gun.

There were ooh's and ahh's and gasps and groans, and finally claps as Mr. McAllister finished his story. He stood up and took a bow; the applause got louder and louder. He was a pretty proud leprechaun cowboy. And I was a pretty proud friend. He turned to me, tipped his hat, and said, "Mighty fine evening, ma'am. Thank ya kindly."

I curtsied. "Mighty fine evening, indeed."

TOO MUCH OF a GOOD THING

I t was early the next morning that I heard the familiar cooing at the window. Rosie was back again with another message from Mr. McAllister. I wondered if he wanted to talk about his wild adventure on Halloween night. Most likely it was something to do with that.

I waved to her from the window. She strutted along the windowsill and seemed to be in no big hurry to leave; she knew there would be a treat for her and she was very patient. I grabbed a handful of pumpkin seeds, threw on my coat and went out back. Rosie fluttered down and stood quietly at my feet while I untied the message.

Dear Big One,

I am hoping for some advice from you.

I ate the candy, almost all of it.

Being a wee bit greedy, I gobbled up all but 23 pieces last night before I went to bed. I'm afraid that was a big mistake. I'm thinkin' it's a good punishment for being selfish, but I've got myself a bad belly ache, and none of our natural potions are workin' to make me feel better. My belly's bigger than a bear and I'm feelin' like one, too. You warned me. I should have listened. It all looked so good and I kept eatin' one, then another, then another. Before I knew it I was bigger than a balloon with a belly-full of ache! Doncha know I'm needin' some help from ya.

Your foolish friend,

Mr. CW McAllister

I felt so sorry for him. He wasn't used to that kind of junk food and he didn't know how yucky you can feel if you've had too much. I had to think of something.

Dear Mr. McAllister,

I'm sorry you're sick. I can't believe you ate that much candy all at once. I warned you, you're right about that. But scolding you won't help your belly ache. I'll be over with something that just might help, a little at least. Put some warm towels on your belly until I get there, and for goodness sake, don't eat anything else!

Love,

Sandy

I sent Rosie off with the message; she was also full from all of her treats. Then, I went inside and made some hot ginger tea, took a handful of peppermint leaves from the garden, chose a book off the shelf, and got in the car for a ride across town. Miss Gloria met me in her driveway and handed me a bag full of cookies. "Sandy,

I have to run some errands, would you mind taking these back to my friend, Mr. McAllister?"

"Oh, Miss Gloria, I'm afraid he's not going to be wanting cookies. He ate nearly all of his Halloween candy last night and this morning he has a very big belly ache. But I'll be happy to give them to the other folks in the village if you'd like. They didn't eat a truckload of candy!"

I took the bag of cookies, the thermos of hot ginger tea, the peppermint leaves, the book, and the cookies and walked down the path to the woods. It was quiet. The children were in school, the pine needles and fallen leaves silenced my steps, and I thought how lovely it was. That is until I heard the groans coming from a doorway up ahead.

"Oh, no. Oh, please, save me. Me belly. Ohhhhhhhh. Burrrp."

It sounded like my brave little cowboy was in some serious pain. "Mr. McAllister. Can you come out here, or send Mrs. McAllister out?"

"Is it you, Big One? I can hardly hear your voice over the rumbling of my achin' belly. No, the Mrs. is over at the Cookin' School teachin' a lesson on stews. I'll try to crawl to the door. Just a minute."

Well I waited and waited, and soon I saw a hand, then another, then a head with a scruffy beard. AND then I saw it. His belly was popping out of his blue plaid shirt, like a beachball ready to explode. He crawled out and stopped at my feet. "Mr. McAllister, you are a mess. You'll be fine in a few hours, but here, you'd better start with this."

I handed him a cup of the ginger tea and sat with him while he sipped it. He said nothing, but every once in a while he'd let out a "Mmmmmm" or a burp, followed quickly by an "Excuse me." This went on for about an hour — Sip some tea, chew some peppermint leaves, burp. Sip some tea, chew some peppermint leaves, burp.

He was feeling a little better, so I asked him if he wanted me to read him a story while he sipped. He thought that would help to pass the time. Before I started,

I left him for a few minutes to deliver the cookies to the Day Care Den. I knew the kids would love a treat from Miss Gloria. Then I stopped at the cooking school to tell Mrs. McAllister that her husband was feeling better and that she shouldn't worry. "That silly old goat," she laughed. "That's what he gets for being a little piggy with all that candy. When I left him this morning he was groaning like a sick cow."

Mr. McAllister was leaning up against the tree when I got back, looking a little better, and he finally had some pink in his cheeks. "Ok," I said, "it's story time. Sit back and listen carefully. I think you might learn a lesson from hearing about a problem someone else had because he ate too much of a good thing." And I began.

"The Tale of Peter Rabbit by Beatrix Potter. Once upon a time..."

THE END

ACKNOWLEDGEMENTS

I'd like to thank the students at schools in Williamsville, New York, who shared their thoughts with me in 2015, before I wrote this book. For those of you who wanted me to write about the duckling adventure – that's next. For those of you who voted for the Halloween adventure, well, I hope you enjoyed it. Your votes were tied, so I picked from a hat and Halloween won.

Thank you to the students at Forest Elementary. It's always fun to visit with you.

Thank you to Mrs. Jacobs' students at Maple East Elementary for being careful listeners.

Thank you to Mrs. Casteel's students at Maple East Elementary. Your letters, questions and discussions were very thoughtful, and the pizza party was so yummy!

Thank you to Mrs. Haubiel's class, also at Maple East. It was exciting to make a surprise visit to your room.

Thank you to Mr. Rhul's class at Maple West Elementary. I still remember what great thinkers you were and what kind hearts you had.

You all helped me with the toughest job an author has... deciding what to write about! Most of all, thank you for inviting me to your classrooms and showing me the magic that only kids can create. You encouraged me, you inspired me, you made my heart smile!

Thank you Angela Stockman for your insightful suggestions. I think Mr. McAllister would like to meet you someday.

And finally, thank you to M&M, Mak and Mark, the talented guys who helped to make it all happen... again!

29869040R00075

Made in the USA
Middletown, DE
05 March 2016